The WHEEL

We're here!

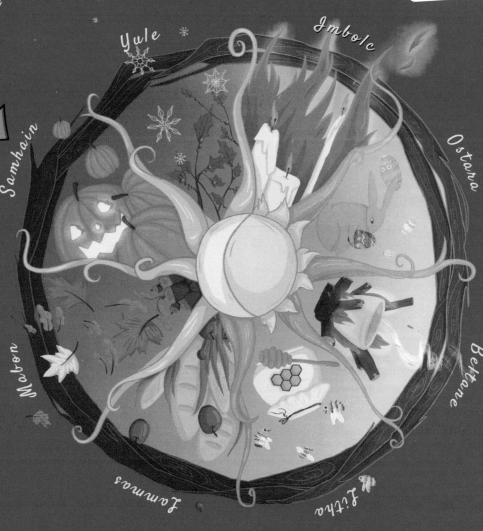

Yule

Imbolc

Ostara

Samhain

Beltane

Mabon

Litha

Lammas

of the YEAR

The last sunset of Summer dips behind the yonder trees,

illuminating crowns of crimson, gold, and orange leaves,

which fall and flutter in the wind before they reach the bottom,

and paint the changing landscape in their lovely shades of Autumn.

As Holly King takes power, Oak King readies for his slumber.

The Groundhog, Snake, and Hare return to Brigid's den down under.

But though the dark is thickening, the veil 'tween worlds grows thin.

O Samhain Night is here at last!

Let revelry begin!

Throughout the town, the village kids get ready for the night,

putting on fantastic costumes, trying to give their friends a fright!

They knock on neighbors' doors, seeking tricks or treats to snag,

then have a pumpkin-carving contest! (The winner gets to **brag**!)

In the field, a wheel of fire sparks ablaze as people cheer,

grateful for the blessings Sun has gifted them this year.

On the quiet side of town, families gather at the graves

of their loved ones now **departed**, but still present in their ways.

On this night, a little spirit somehow found themself awake

in a graveyard lit by candles, decked in ornaments and cakes.

The other graves had all been visited by family and friends

who'd come to greet their ancestors and spend more time with them.

The little spirit frowned to see that their own grave was bare.

Had no one come to visit them?

Was there anyone who cared?

Just then, the spirit realized that they could not recall any name, or face, or memory of any life at all!

The little spirit shivered, feeling frightened and alone.

"No kin has come, and I am lost!" the little spirit moaned.

From a nearby bowl of **offerings** rose eyes of yellow-green,

where a cat as black as midnight stepped out into the scene.

"Follow me," said cat to spirit, with a grin upon its face,

"If you're wishing to remember, then I know just the place!".

The little spirit followed, having hope the cat was right,
but grew nervous as they traveled through the eerie trails of night.

The **feline** ran like lightning, as he would chasing a mouse,

until, at last, he stopped to lick his paws beside a house.

The home was small but **charming** on a field of fallen leaves

with its doors and windows open, letting in the Autumn breeze.

"There's something quite familiar here," the little spirit said

and peeked within to find a most delightful dinner spread.

The scene was warm and welcoming, so spirit went inside,

when suddenly they heard a loving **choir** shout, "Surprise!"

A lifetime full of memories came rushing back, at last!

The little spirit recognized each loved one from her past!

Welcome home, Mom!" sang her daughter.

"Nana's back!" her grandson cheered.

Then Grandpa kissed her hand and whispered,

"You've been missed, my dear."

That night, the family once again

shared laughs and tears together,

for as the Samhain promise goes:

Family is forever.

Glossary

Ancestors: a person in your family who lived a long time ago

Brag: to talk too proudly about something you own or something you have done

Charming: very pleasant or attractive

Choir: a group of people who sing together

Crimson: a dark red color

Decked: to decorate somebody or something

Departed: a person who has died

Eerie: strange, mysterious and frightening

Feline: a cat

Illuminated: lit with bright lights

Kin: family, relatives

Landscape: what you can see when you look across a large area of land

Offerings: something that is given to a god or spirit to honor them

Ornaments: an object that is used as decoration

Revelry: noisy fun, usually involving a lot of eating and drinking

About the Sabbat

Samhain (pronounced SOW-EN) is an autumn sabbat celebrated on October 31st in the Northern Hemisphere, and on May 1st in the Southern Hemisphere. It marks the end of the last harvest of the year. Fields are now bare. Grey skies are bringing in colder winds, which blow away the last leaves from their branches. It's now the "dark half" of the year, where the sun is weakest, and the earth begins to die (really, it's just a deep sleep).

Similar to Beltane, this is the second time of year that the veil between our world and the spirit world is thinnest. Samhain is a time to honor loved ones who have passed and to reconnect with our ancestors. Some families visit the graves of loved ones, decorating the space with flowers, candles, treats, and other offerings. Other families might hold a "dumb supper," where both the living and the dead are able to feast together. Some skilled individuals may even hold a séance, a way of communicating with the dearly departed!

Samhain vs. Halloween

Like some other pagan sabbats, which share similarities with Christian and non-pagan holidays (Easter = Ostara, Yule = Christmas), Halloween also has pagan roots. In fact, many of its traditions, like putting on costumes and going trick-or-treating started several hundred years ago! In some earlier pagan traditions, dressing up in costume was a way to hide oneself from any evil spirits or Fae that roamed the earth looking for trouble on this night. In other places, villagers would dress up as the souls of the dead and went door-to-door collecting food for their Samhain feasts. In parts of Scotland, pranks (tricks) became so popular among groups of youths that it became known as "Mischief Night."

Talk about a TRICK or TREAT!

celebrate Samhain!

Below are some family-friendly ways to celebrate the sabbat.

Happy Witches' New Year!

In Celtic traditions, Samhain is celebrated as the Witches' New Year. It's a time to say goodbye to the old and welcome in the new. Share toasts of cider with loved ones, recalling lessons of the past year and the milestones ahead. Have a countdown for midnight (earlier for younger witchlings) and together shout "Happy Witches' New Year!"

Honor Your Ancestors

Set up your family altar with symbols of the fall season and the Samhain sabbat, like dried leaves, apples, pumpkins, or even plastic spiders, skulls and bats! Make sure to leave a space to place pictures of your departed family members, even items they may have once used and cherished. Place a plate or cup with an offering of some of the treats your family will be enjoying together this night. Spend some time sharing stories of those who have crossed over. At dinnertime, remember to set up an extra place setting for them!

Get Spooky with it!

Since Samahin shares ties with Halloween, it can get kinda spooky at times. But that's part of the fun! Gather your bravest friends and family members and take turns sharing ghost stories and frightful tales around the fire or the glow of a flashlight. Make one up, or choose a spook-tacular book for a haunting read-aloud.!

Carve a Jack-o-lantern

Pick your favorite pumpkin from the patch or grocery store and some kid-safe carving tools to create one of the most fun traditions of the season: the jack-o-lantern! Try using paint, markers, or stickers to make your pumpkin unique. You can even draw or carve magical runes and symbols on its surface to invite blessings in the new year. Invite your friends and have a pumpkin carving contest!

Make a Family Tree

Another way to connect with your ancestors is by researching and creating a family tree chart. A family tree chart is a visual way to see how each generation is connected, from the roots to the leaves. Together with the help of older family members, create an outline that traces back as far as they can remember. Write names and dates on the leaves of the tree. Once you have completed your family tree, add it to your family altar!

Word Scramble

Unscramble the words below to correctly spell the glossary terms.

errveyl _____

grba _____

filnee _____

tliieluandm _____

reffgoisn _____

tsroseacn _____

graihcnm _____

ink _____

icorh _____

kdedce _____

ntmoasner _____

Match the Meaning

Write each glossary word below the image that best matches its meaning.

illuminate   crimson   lanscape   revelry
departed   ornaments   feline   ancestors

_____   _____   _____   _____

_____   _____   _____   _____

Match the Meaning

Write each glossary word below the image that best matches its meaning.

> offerings   choir   charming
>
> brag   decked   eerie   kin

_____   _____   _____   _____

_____   _____   _____

Vocabulary Fill-in-the-Blank

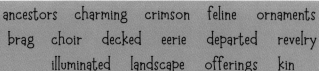

Use the glossary words in the word bank to fill the blanks in the sentences below. You can only use each word once.

ancestors	charming	crimson	feline	ornaments
brag	choir	decked	eerie	departed	revelry
illuminated	landscape	offerings	kin	

1. I don't mean to _____, but I'm the best pumpkin-carver that ever lived!

2. Although some of them are pets, a _____ can also be loved as if they were your own _____.

3. The gold and _____ leaves on the trees were _____ by the sun's light.

4. The _____ of the countryside was colorful and _____ during the daylight hours.

5. Nighttime shadows can make a place feel spooky and _____.

6. To honor their _____, families place _____ upon the graves of their dearly _____ loved ones.

7. The family _____ their home with candles, banners, and _____ in celebration of Samhain night.

8. We could hear the _____ singing and the sounds of _____ from the Autumn Festival down the street.

SAMHAIN

Acrostic Poem

S _____

A _____

M _____

H _____

A _____

I _____

N _____

Writing Prompt

Samhain is a time to honor our loved ones who are no longer with us in the mortal realm. One way we keep their memory alive is through storytelling. Use the space below to tell the story of one of your ancestors, celebrating who they were and the life they lived. You can ask an older family member about them for more details. You can also use your imagination and make up a story about an ancestor that might have lived a long, long time ago! Draw or attach a photo of your chosen ancestor on the picture frame at the bottom of the page..

_____

_____

_____

_____

_____

_____

_____

_____

_____

_____

_____

_____

_____

_____

My Samhain Masterpiece

Color and draw on the pumpkin below to create your own spook-tacular Jack-o-lantern!

The SONGS of SABBATS

- Imbolg: Bright's Feast — Alexandre Ravenhart
- Ostara at the Hare — Alexandre Ravenhart
- Beltane and the Fairy Flame — Alexandre Ravenhart
- Litha: — Alexandre Ravenhart
- Lammas and the First Fruits — Alexandre Ravenhart
- Mabon and the Land of Night — Alexandre Ravenhart
- Samhain and the Lost Spirit — Alexandre Ravenhart
- Yule: a Winter's Wassail — Alexandre Ravenhart

All books in this series are available on Amazon!

Follow @AlexandreRavenhart on Instagram for updates and upcoming projects! Visit the **author's website** below for merchandise from the series!

Merry Part!
Until we merry meet again!
-A. Ravenhart

alexandreravenhart.wixsite.com/blog

Printed in Great Britain
by Amazon